JACK-O'-LANTERN

JACK-

Third Printing

Text copyright © 1974 by Edna Barth
Pictures copyright © 1974 by Paul Galdone

Printed in the United States of America

Library of Congress Cataloging in Publication Data

Barth, Edna.
  Jack-o'-lantern.
    SUMMARY: Retells the story of the first jack-o'-lantern, made to light
the way of Mean Jack who, unwanted in heaven and hell, had to wander
the earth for eternity.
    [1. Folklore. 2. Halloween—Fiction] I. Galdone, Paul, illus. II. Title.
PZ8.1.B3Jac   [398.2] [E]   73-20194
ISBN 0-8164-3120-5

-LANTERN

by Edna Barth

Pictures by Paul Galdone

A Clarion Book

The Seabury Press
New York

Have you ever heard the story
of the first jack-o'-lantern?
It goes like this:

ONCE, many years ago, up in the hills
around Littleboro, there was a blacksmith who was so
mean and cussed they called him Mean Jack. If Jack's
wife Sairy Ann needed money for a spool of cotton
thread, he'd cuss and fume for a week before he'd
give it to her. Then he'd cuss and fume for another
week after he had. He wouldn't give a neighbor a
hand with anything, not even a barn raising, and it
nearly killed him to have to lend anybody a tool.

Mean Jack never went to meeting for fear he'd have to part with a few coppers for the collection plate. The Reverend Crawford came up from the valley once and gave him a talking to. "When you die, Jack," he said, "what do you suppose will become of your soul?"

Mean Jack laughed right in his face. He didn't give a hang for anybody, not even the preacher, and he cared even less about his soul.

One cold night, about the middle of January, Jack and Sairy Ann were sitting before the fire, trying to get warm. Sleet was hammering against the window-panes, and wind was howling around the eaves and blowing in through every cranny. All of a sudden there came a knock at the kitchen door.

"What kind of a fool would be abroad on a night like this?" grumbled Jack, getting up from his place by the fire.

On the step stood a frail, white-haired old man. He shivered and shook so much that it was a minute or two before he could speak. Then he managed to whisper, "My good man, give me a night's lodging and something to eat, I beg you."

Jack was going to slam the door in his face, but, through a hole in the old man's ragged coat, he saw the gleam of something that looked like gold. "Well, I guess you can come in, old man," he said.

Sairy Ann nearly fainted.

The old man was seated before the fire and given
a plateful of food—some of Saturday's baked beans
warmed up, bread spread thick with Sairy's butter, a

mug of milk, and a wedge of pie. Jack and Sairy watched him eat it.

The poor fellow was so weak he could hardly lift his fork. But when he finished he seemed different somehow. He looked younger and stronger and there was a kind of light all around him.

He put down his plate, took off his ragged coat, and got up. There he stood, with his flowing hair and white robe. Around his waist was a golden cord with a big gold key hanging from it.

"I guess you know who I am, Jack," said St. Peter, for that's who he was.

"Of course I do," said Mean Jack. "What do you take me for, a numbskull?"

If St. Peter was surprised he didn't show it. "It's like this, Jack," he said, "One of my jobs is up above, tending the gates of heaven. Another one is checking up on folks down here. When I can spare the time I come down disguised as a beggar. I wander around, and anyone that takes me in, I give 'em three wishes."

"You don't say so!" said Mean Jack, with a big wink at Sairy Ann.

"Jack!" Sairy Ann warned in a frightened whisper. She might have been a chunk of firewood for all the notice he paid her.

"Yes, Jack," said St. Peter. "I heard tell how mean and cussed you were, but look at the way you took me in tonight. Folks must be wrong about you or else you've changed a lot—one or the other."

Mean Jack just grinned as if St. Peter were some old fool.

"Well . . ." said St. Peter, taking out a big gold watch, "I must be on my way. So go to it, son. Make your three wishes."

"Make my three wishes," said Jack, mocking St. Peter's very tone. Then he named the first thing that came into his head. "Out in my blacksmith shop there's an old rocking chair. Seems as if every time I turn around, some idler is sitting in it. I wish that anybody I catch in that rocker would sit and rock 'till I let 'em go."

St. Peter was taken aback, but he tried to hide it. "All right, Jack," he said. "Now what's your second wish?"

"Well," said Jack, and he named the next thing that came into his head. "Seems as if every time I turn

my back, someone begins fiddling with my bellows—
just for the sport of seeing the sparks fly. I'd like anyone who touches my bellows to stick fast to 'em as long
as I say so. That's my second wish."

St. Peter was too flabbergasted to speak at first. "Only one more wish to go," he said at last. "If I was you, I'd give it some thought, son."

But Mean Jack went right ahead and named the next thing that came into his head. "Down below my blacksmith shop there's a big apple tree—bears the best Baldwins for miles around. Every fall I catch people helping themselves." His voice shook. "I'd like to see anybody who climbs my apple tree stuck fast 'till I let 'em down. That's my third wish."

"Your third and last," snapped St. Peter. "Your wishes will be granted, but you've gone and wasted them, I can tell you that. You should have wished for the good of your soul."

"The good of my soul!" scoffed Mean Jack.

St. Peter stood shaking his head and looking at Jack for a minute or two. Then he vanished. *Poufff!*

Sairy Ann gave a start, but Jack chuckled, "Well, I got the best of him, didn't I?"

After that, Jack got meaner and more cussed than ever. Idlers found better places to pass their time than in his blacksmith shop, and people who had him shoe their horses or mend their tools hurried away from him as fast as they could.

"That Jack!" they said. "He's nearly as mean as the Devil."

The Devil heard about it from a tin pedlar who had lost his way and ended up in the deep hollow where Hell was.

"Almost as mean as me!" snorted the Devil. "We'll see about that. Norman!" he called out to his youngest and smallest son. "You go up and fetch me that blacksmith!"

The next morning Mean Jack was pounding away at his anvil when a movement at the window caught his eye. There, peering in at him, was a creature about the size of a woodchuck.

The window opened and the little fellow hopped inside. "Morning," he said, planting himself in front of Jack. "Pa says you're to come home with me."

"All right." Jack pretended to humor him. "We'll be off in a twinkling. But first I must finish shaping an axle for this wheelbarrow. Have to strike while the iron is hot, you know."

"Strike while the iron is hot! Strike while the iron is hot!" chanted the little devil. He was a merry sort. At each clang of Jack's hammer he jumped up and down in time.

Then, tiring of that, the little devil hopped into Jack's rocker. Holding onto the arms, he rocked so hard he nearly turned over. But when he got tired of rocking and tried to stop, he found he couldn't. "Mr. Blacksmith," he called, "stop this chair from rocking. I want to get out of it."

Mean Jack just laughed and let him go on rocking, with his head going bang-bang-bang against the back.

"Let me go!" wailed the little devil. "Let me go!"

When Jack saw that he'd had his fill, he said, "If you promise to clear out of here and never come back, I'll let you go."

"I promise! I promise!" screamed the little devil, so Jack let him go.

The poor little devil ran off down the road, yelling his head off. He never came back, either.

As time went on, Jack got meaner and more cussed still. He would finish mending a mattock for a farmer and then fling it at him. "Here," he'd say. "Give me a quarter of a dollar, take your mattock, and git!"

He was the only blacksmith for miles around. Otherwise no one would ever have had him do a bit of work for them.

"That Jack!" they said. "He's as mean and cussed as the very Devil!"

Now the Devil had never yet met his match for meanness, so he didn't like this one bit when he heard it. Sparks flew from his eyes, and his tail gave an angry lash.

His missus could see that Mean Jack was beginning to irritate him. "Go on up and fetch him down here where you can keep track of him," she suggested.

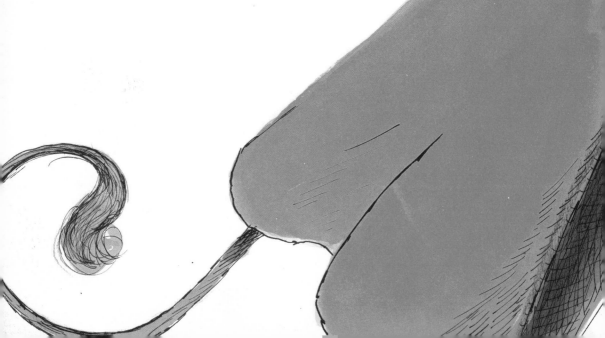

"I will not," said the Devil. "It's beneath me."

"Then send Everett."

So the Devil called out
to Everett, his oldest son.
"You go up there and get
the blacksmith they call Jack.
He seems to think
he's as mean as me."

Toward evening that same day Jack was pumping the handle of his big bellows when a movement at
the window caught his eye. There, peering in at him,
was a devil, a good deal bigger than the first one.

"Evening," the young devil said. "Pa sent me up
to fetch you."

"Come in, son," said Mean Jack. "I'll be with
you in a jiffy. Have to finish up this one horseshoe.
Then we'll be off."

So the young devil came in and walked around,
looking at everything in Jack's shop. He was the
curious sort.

After a while, though, he began to get fidgety. "Let me work the bellows for you," he said to Jack, "and you take the tongs. That way you'll be finished sooner. Pa told me not to linger."

Of course Jack was delighted and agreed to it right away.

The flames leapt upward, and bright sparks went flying in all directions. "Ready now," said the son of the Devil when the fire was at its brightest and hottest.

Jack grasped his tongs and thrust the horseshoe into the fire. As soon as it turned from a cherry red to a glowing white, he took it to the anvil. He was swinging his sledgehammer to pound the hot shoe into shape, when the young devil began yelling.

"These bellows of yours are devilish! I can't stop them from working—can't even let go of them! They won't let go of *me*!"

Jack gave one of his meanest laughs. "You bet your life they won't!" he said as he plunged the horseshoe into the dousing tub.

From the corner of his eye, Jack watched the Devil's son. He was stuck fast to the bellows handle, his arms pumping up and down, up and down, above his head. And he was roaring like a young bull.

Jack let him go on like that for quite a while. Then he made him an offer. "Give me your word that you'll clear out of here and never come back, and I'll let you go."

"I give you my word! I give you my word!" yelled the young devil.

So Mean Jack let him go, and he streaked off down the road, roaring his head off. He never came back, either.

In time, Jack got so mean and cussed that people dreaded the thought of going near him. They put off having their horses shod or their tools mended as long as they could.

"That Jack!" they said. "He's meaner than the Devil himself!"

When the Devil heard this, he turned from a bright red to a deep purple. "We'll see about that!" he bellowed. Sparks flew from his eyes and flames poured out of both nostrils.

This time, instead of sending up one of his sons, he decided to go himself. "For I'll not be outdone!" he said.

"Calm down," advised his missus, "and while you're up there, keep your wits about you. That black-smith is a hard one to outdo."

It was a mild day, toward the end of September.
Jack was working away on the tines of a pitchfork
when he noticed a shadow on the smithy floor.

He looked up, and
there at the door
was the Devil himself,
holding a pitchfork
of his own.

"Jack the Blacksmith," the Devil said, and he planted one of his cloven hoofs inside the door. "You're to come with me now!" His eyes were like two stones.

Jack could see the Devil meant business. "I'll be with you in no time," he said. "Just have to give this pitchfork a lick and a promise. Told a man over to Hancock I'd have it ready for him this afternoon. Make yourself right at home in that rocker there."

"I will not!" The Devil started to lose his temper, then caught himself. "I left my missus tending the fires," he explained. "If I'm gone too long, she'll get cranky."

"Oh, I see," said Jack meekly. "Well, we'll be off in two shakes if you'll just work the bellows while I . . ."

"I'll do nothing of the kind!"

The floorboards trembled as the Devil came striding forward. His eyes were blazing. The veins in his neck looked close to bursting. Another step and he and Jack stood face to face.

Suddenly Jack jumped aside to the right, but the Devil jumped aside to the right, too.

They circled around like that until the Devil stood facing the door. Jack could tell he was ready to spring.

Then all at once he lost interest. Through the open door he had spotted Jack's Baldwin apple tree. It seems the Devil had a weakness for apples and liked a good Baldwin best of all.

"Help yourself," said Jack, seeing him eye the apples. "They're all mighty good Baldwins, but the biggest and best ones are up near the top."

The Devil gave him a suspicious glare. Then his eyes went back to the apple tree, loaded from top to bottom with bright red fruit. "Stay where you are," he said to Jack. "Make a move, and it will be the end of you." And in two seconds he was out the door and up in the tree.

Jack could hear him crunching away on one apple after another, making sure that he got the best. The ground below was soon peppered with black seeds.

Finally he had his fill and started down, dropping nimbly from limb to limb. Now he was ready to drop to the ground.

Jack nearly died laughing as he watched his face.

First the Devil tried to let himself down by taking the lowest limb in both hands. Then he tried sitting down on it, intending to jump. Next he tried standing up, as if to dive. No matter what he did he stuck fast to the lowest limb.

"Help me down out of this fiendish tree!" The Devil fumed and cussed and named the terrible things he would do to Jack if he refused.

Mean Jack left the Devil yelling his head off
and went back to his shop. When passersby heard all
the fuming and cussing, they thought it was Jack
himself.

"That Jack!" they said, shaking their heads.
"The Devil himself couldn't be meaner or more
cussed."

At suppertime Jack went into the house, washed
up, and ate his meal. After supper he wound the
clock, put the cat out, and got ready for bed.

"What do you suppose all that racket is down by
the apple tree?" asked Sairy Ann.

Mean Jack didn't even bother to answer, but
Sairy Ann was used to that so she turned over and
went to sleep.

As Jack drifted off to sleep himself, he thought
with a chuckle, "We'll see how his lordship looks at
things come tomorrow morning."

At sunrise he went out to investigate. There
wasn't so much as a peep from the Baldwin apple tree.
Then a pitiful little voice called, "Mr. Blacksmith?"

"Oh," said Jack, "you mean to say you're still up there?"

"Yes," said the Devil, "and I'd give a good deal to get down, too."

"Would you now?" said Jack. "Well, well! If I let you down, how long will you stay away from here?"

"Five years," said the Devil.

"Five years!" Mean Jack spat on the ground.

"Ten, then," offered the Devil.

"Ten years!" Mean Jack spat again.

They dickered some more and Mean Jack got the Devil up to fifty years. By that time he was tired of his joke, for that's all it was, so he said, "You promise to go away from here and never come back, and I'll let you down from my tree."

"It's a bargain," gasped the Devil, so used up he could hardly make it to the ground.

Once down, he gathered himself together and slunk away, his tail dragging in the dust of the road.

Not long after that Mean Jack got all used up himself. Around All Hallows Eve he died. Sairy Ann didn't mourn him very much, and nobody blamed her for it, either.

As for Jack, no sooner was he buried than he climbed up out of his grave. Taking his sledgehammer, he set off for the crossroads where one road led to Heaven and one to Hell.

While he was getting his bearings, along came a blind man with his begging cup still in his hand.

"Where do you think you're going?" demanded Jack.

The blind man looked frightened. "To Heaven," he said, "if they'll have me there."

"Then we might as well go together," said Jack, planning to sneak inside when the gate was opened for the blind man.

It was quite a distance to Heaven but the two of them finally got there. "You can be first," Jack said. He shoved the blind man toward the golden gates. Then, from behind a bush, he watched the man march up, knock, and give his name.

St. Peter looked up the name in a big golden book. "All right," he said, "you can come in."

The gate creaked open, and before it closed, Jack hurled in his sledgehammer to keep it ajar.

"Oh, no you don't!" St. Peter kicked the sledge-hammer out of the way. "I remember you!" He slammed the gate shut. "You're Mean Jack, and we have no room for you here!"

Now there was nothing Jack could do but turn around and head for Hell. It was quite a distance from Heaven, but along toward evening he finally got there.

The Devil's young ones were all over the front porch and dooryard, yelling, fighting, and up to deviltry of all kinds. The Devil's missus sat rocking.

Then Norman noticed Jack and tugged at his mother's sleeve. "Mean Jack is coming!"

His mother looked up the road and gasped. "Go get Papa!"

When Jack drew near, the Devil was out fitting a big padlock onto the gate.

"What's that for?" asked Jack. "I thought you wanted me down here."

"I should say not," the Devil replied. "You're so mean you'd have the whole place turned upside down in fifteen minutes."

"Then where can I go?" asked Mean Jack. "St. Peter doesn't want any part of me either. There must be someplace I can go for the rest of eternity."

The Devil leered at him through the fence pickets. "For the rest of eternity," he said, "you can go chasing yourself from one place to another—so git!"

"But it's dark out here," Jack complained. "If I can't see myself, how can I chase myself?"

The Devil thought that one over. Then he picked up his tongs and plucked a hot coal from the nearest furnace. "Here." He tossed the coal over the fence. "You can take this to light your way."

"Anything to get rid of him," the Devil explained to his young ones.

As they watched, Jack ran his hand over the ground until he came to a good sized pumpkin. This he hollowed out, carving a few holes on one side. Then he dropped the glowing coal into the pumpkin. With this strange lantern to light his way, Mean Jack went wandering off.

And so he has wandered ever since. Perhaps you've seen him. He appears as a little light bobbing along over a swamp or marsh at night.

Some speak of the flickering light as a will-o-the-wisp. Some say it is nothing but marsh gas. That's only because they don't know about Mean Jack and what happened to him on All Hallows Eve so long ago.

But you and I know.

Author's Note

Searching for material on the jack-o'-lantern for my book *Witches, Pumpkins, and Grinning Ghosts: The Story of the Halloween Symbols*, I came upon a fascinating bit of Irish folklore. It was the fragmentary story of Stingy Jack who, on two successive Halloweens, tricked the Devil into sparing his soul. When he died, turned back both at Heaven and Hell and condemned to wander the earth for eternity, he begged for something to light his way. The Devil grudgingly tossed him a glowing coal. Stingy Jack hollowed out a turnip, carved some holes in it, and put the hot coal inside.

It seemed to me that this fragment, expanded, might make an interesting Halloween story. Because I wanted to use authentic folklore motifs rather than invented ones, I consulted *The Motif Index of Folk Literature* by Stith Thompson.

Among the many Devil tales was one that involved a blacksmith. In varying forms it has been told all over Europe. Probably brought to the New World by English settlers, it has cropped up in the oral tradition of North Carolina, Virginia, Maryland, Kentucky, and perhaps other areas.

As *Wicked John and the Devil*, it appears in Richard Chase's *Grandfather Tales*. Parallels are also found in *Grimm's Tales*, in Joel Chandler Harris' *Uncle Remus* stories, and in Zora Hurston's *Mules and Men*.

Most versions contain elements from antiquity, when gods were thought to walk the earth at times. All have elements from the Middle Ages, when people being tried for witchcraft were accused of making pacts or bargains with the Devil.

Usually a blacksmith, Jack is sometimes a drunkard, sometimes a miser, and sometimes a hardpressed man forced to deal with the Devil for the sake of his family. In versions that include the three wishes, an angel sometimes replaces St. Peter. Sometimes St. Peter accompanies Christ. The three wishes vary, too. In some versions the smith wishes for a steel purse in which to capture anyone small enough to creep into it. The apple tree of *Jack-o'-Lantern* is sometimes a sycamore, a pear tree, or a thorn bush.

In most tales the Devil comes for Jack by himself, but in several he sends emissaries or comes accompanied by all his little devils. When some of the versions of Celtic origin were written down, the jack-o'-lantern element was added on.

I have told my version in the idiom of my native New England, basing Jack's character on a New Englander I remember hearing described as "the meanest cuss in town."

—Edna Barth

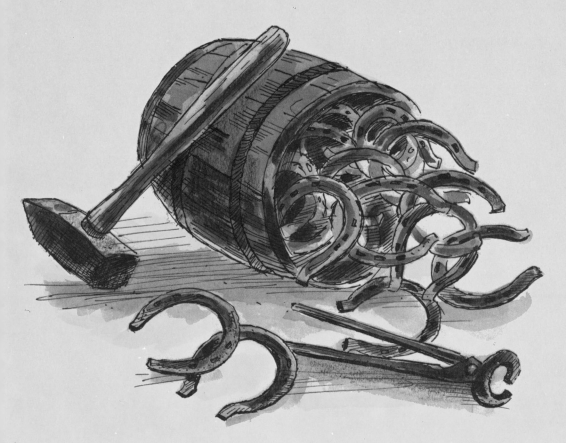

ABOUT THE AUTHOR

Edna Barth received a B.A. from Radcliffe College and a B.S. from the School of Library Science at Simmons College. She has worked as a librarian and teacher, and today is an editor of books for young people in New York City.

Mrs. Barth is the author of a number of young people's books, including *I'm Nobody! Who Are You? The Story of Emily Dickinson* and her well-received group of books on the symbols of Easter, Christmas, Halloween, and Valentine's Day.

ABOUT THE ARTIST

Paul Galdone spends much time on his Vermont farm. The rough, rustic charm and accurate detail found in his illustrations for *Jack-O'-Lantern* reflect his knowledge of the New England countryside and its people.

Paul Galdone has contributed many outstanding picture books to the Seabury list. Most recently his interpretation of *The Little Red Hen* appeared on *School Library Journal's* "Best Books of 1973" list and was also an A.L.A. Notable Children's Book.